Published by Tate Publishing & Enterprises, LLC
127 E. Trade Center Terrace | Mustang, Oklahoma 73064 USA
1.888.361.9473 | www.tatepublishing.com

Tate Publishing is committed to excellence in the publishing industry. The company reflects the philosophy established by the founders, based on Psalm 68:11,
"The Lord gave the word and great was the company of those who published it."

Book design copyright © 2011 by Tate Publishing, LLC. All rights reserved.
Cover & Interior design by Stephanie Woloszyn
Illustrations by Kael Little

Published in the United States of America

ISBN: 978-1-61777-758-5
Juvenile Fiction / Animals / Farm Animals
11.06.27

Dedication

To Lexy, Tyler, Julia, Sammi, Lily,
Frankie, Beebs, and Alyssa,
the best grandchildren in the world

Acknowledgments

I am especially thankful to the animals in these stories who helped to create the tales with their unique personalities and actions. Most of all, however, I thank God for his inspiration and guidance. Without Him, this endeavor would not have been possible.

Table of Contents

PROLOGUE

Welcome to Castle Hill Acres and the royal subjects who reside here. As you begin reading, it is another beautiful day filled with golden sunlight, shimmering reflections in the bright blue stream, and dark green forest trees that seem to whisper, "Hello." As King Flash, a cherished and beloved horse, strolls through the emerald green meadows, his wish is to share these stories of incredible love with you and to let you know that all the animals have a purpose in life. May their purposes serve you well, and may you enjoy your time in the castle.

A NAUGHTY CAT LEARNS ABOUT LOVE

A majestic house and stable, known as Castle Hill Acres, regally stood among hills and forests in Pennsylvania. The stable housed many animals, including different colored horses and three cats: Princess Flower, Prince Smitty, and the Queen of Ugly, NC, otherwise known as Naughty Cat, who, more often than not, never seemed to learn how to be sociable and kind and who never wanted to love others. Unfortunately, she did not have any friends either.

The owners were very fond of their animals and showered them with lots of love; thus, the animals were all sweet and lovable, except, of course, for NC, who did not seem to like her owners either. Princess Flower was a tiny, yet beautiful Calico cat who snuggled with her

owners and was kind to all the mice and birds. She never ever was mean-spirited or unhappy.

Prince Smitty was a fat black cat who loved to eat. In fact, he often ate at other people's houses too. He loved to hunt and always guarded the owners' property. He never let strange cats come into the stable and delighted in being "the big furry hunter." Smitty loved everybody, too, and he was never rude or nasty.

One night, NC pranced into the stable to eat her supper at the usual time when no humans were around. They would have scolded her for picking on Princess Flower and Prince Smitty. NC thought she was in charge of everything and was never afraid to express her opinion or show her claws. This particular night, Princess Flower was eating some delicious tuna fish that her owners had given her as a treat. NC swatted at Flower and said some hateful things that should not to be repeated. Poor Princess Flower ran across the barn and hid in the hay. She was crying when Prince Smitty arrived on the scene.

"What have you done now?" he yelled at NC.

"Why, whatever are you talking about, little boy? I have not done anything, and I am ready to enjoy my wonderful treat. *So* there!"

"Well, you must have done something to make poor little Flower cry."

NC looked down her stubby, fluffy grey and white nose and said, "Listen, little boy. I don't need to be bothered by you. I have much better things to do. Don't you need to go and hunt for a living?"

With that, NC finished Flower's tuna treat, and with an attitude that she was the most highly valued cat on the acres, she curled up on a soft blanket and promptly fell asleep.

In the meantime, King Flash, the wisest and oldest horse in the stable, heard everything and was very upset. He decided that NC needed to be taught a big lesson, and he was going to give her one. First, however, he said to Princess Flower, "There, there, my little one. I will fix everything that is wrong. Please don't worry about anything and try to get some sleep." Flash, you see, was, indeed, a powerful black and white steed that ran the stable with fairness and love. The last thing he would tolerate was nastiness.

"Prince Smitty," he said in his very deep voice, "we need to teach that bad cat a good lesson."

"I agree," meowed Prince Smitty. "What should we do, King Flash?"

"I am not sure at the moment, but I will think of something soon. While I am thinking, please hug Princess Flower and tell her not to worry." With that, Prince Smitty smiled and purred.

Now, you need to understand that King Flash was locked inside his stall, so he had to think of a highly ingenious plan. Of course, he would need to enlist the help of Prince Smitty, the fat cat himself, and maybe the mice and birds. All night long, King Flash thought and thought and planned and planned. He paced around in circles, swished his long, silky tail, and barely slept a wink. Finally, around dawn, he thought of a plan!

Some other, not-so-elegant members of the stable included Pokey the possum, Martin the mouse, and Barry the bat. They were all a bit crafty and always liked adventure themselves,

so King Flash thought they would be assets to the plan. They also loved Princess Flower, as she was always kind and loving to them as well. Naturally, they agreed with King Flash to help (he was much bigger than they), and they loved a challenge.

The next evening as the owners were feeding King Flash, Prince Smitty waited for the perfect opportunity. After the owners put hay in the king's stall, Prince Smitty distracted them by crying out and holding up his left paw. "Oh, it hurts," cried Smitty. The truth was that he did have problems with his paw, so the owners did not question his behavior. He limped over to the water dish and rolled over on his back. The owners were so worried that they forgot to close the king's door all the way. Later, after the owners left, King Flash called Pokey and Martin to help him.

"They didn't latch the door, but I need you to help me open it," he bellowed. Immediately, Pokey and Martin went to work and tugged and tugged until the door was opened enough so that King Flash could open it the rest of the way with his strong nose. Now all everyone had to do was wait until NC made an appearance.

Around midnight, in marched the naughty, little cat, with her tail proudly swaying in the air and with a pleased look on her face. She just loved to be the center of attention and better and prettier than anyone else. How she hated Pokey and Martin, not to mention Barry the bat. Anyway, she trotted over to the feed dish only to discover that Pokey was eating her food.

"Get out of the way, you miserable rat," she exclaimed.

"Oh, you will be sorry that you said that," piped Pokey.

"Whatever," quipped NC, "I don't need to pay attention to the likes of you."

With that, Barry swooped down, grabbed NC by the neck, and flew with her across to the other side of the stable.

"Put me down, you miserable rodent!" NC screeched.

"No problem, Missy," replied the bat.

With that, he dropped her at the feet of the impressive King Flash. Now, you must remember that King Flash was never out of the stall when NC was around, so this came as quite a shock to her.

"Oh, oh, h-how d-did this h-happen?" she gulped. All of a sudden, however, she remembered to be better than anyone else and said, "Get lost, big boy. You don't scare me."

With that, King Flash put his face down next to hers and showed all his big white teeth (although he was really smiling, NC thought he was going to bite her), and with that, her hair stood on end and she crouched and growled.

"So, Naughty Cat, we meet at last. I guess you are surprised that I am out of my stall. Now nothing can stop me from teaching you a valuable lesson. You do remember who is in charge here, do you not?"

"I suppose," replied the arrogant cat.

King Flash bellowed again, "Why are you so mean and nasty? Don't you understand that being kind to others is what we teach in this stable?"

"I guess," NC said with a smirk on her face.

"I will not tolerate this kind of behavior ever again, or I shall banish you from our humble abode. Is that clear?"

At this point, NC was a bit afraid of the huge horse but was still determined to defy him.

"Yes, Big Flash, I promise to never be unkind again," NC retorted.

With that, Barry swooped down once again, grabbed her by the scruff of the neck, and flew back to the other side of the barn. NC, a bit frightened by this sudden turn of events, raced to leave the stable and promptly ran into the stable door instead of running through the cat opening. Poor NC lay still and lifeless as King Flash and everyone else ran to her aid. Princess Flower was the first on the scene and begged Martin and Pokey to carry her back to the hay. With as much strength as they could muster, the creatures lifted the lifeless form and moved her to her new bed.

All through the night, Princess Flower snuggled up to her to keep her warm, while Prince Smitty brought his treats and some water for her to drink if she awakened. King Flash was not happy with this turn of events, but he decided that something good would definitely result.

The next morning before feeding, NC awakened with a startled meow. She was very sore, and her head ached terribly. Flower licked her head and put her sweet little paws around NC's neck.

"I will take care of you so that you will get better soon," purred Princess Flower.

NC, who was still too sick to answer, just nodded her head as she drifted back to sleep.

"Oh, King Flash," cried Flower, "do you think she will be well soon?"

King Flash, with all of his years of wisdom, replied, "I know she will be better in three days. Please don't fret, little one."

For three days and nights, Smitty, Flower, Martin, Barry, and Pokey helped to brush NC's long, silky hair, feed her all of their treats, and sing songs to lift her spirits. NC watched as the animals laughed and talked and loved each other. She also could not believe that they were so kind to her when she had been nothing but miserable to them. *Perhaps,* she thought, *this is the way I should act towards others.*

Finally, the day came when NC was feeling much better. King Flash asked that the others bring her to him for a meeting. NC was terrified.

"Now, Miss NC, how are you today?" inquired Flash.

"I am much better, sir," responded NC.

"What have you learned from this?"

"Well, sir," NC said in a shaky voice, "I have learned that being nice to others is so much better than being rude. I also like having friends. I was so lonely before. I just hope that I can be as good a friend as they are."

King Flash replied with a friendly snort, "Good, NC, I will be watching and listening. Don't forget that rules are meant to be kept, is that clear?"

"Y-yes, sir," replied the quivering cat.

With that King Flash winked at the others and, with a flourish of his black and white tail, strolled out to the pasture.

NC certainly learned her lesson, for as far as we know today, she has been a really good cat (some even call her GC now), and she is very polite. And on an even happier note, Princess Flower has a beautiful new friend.

A STORMY NIGHT SAVES TWO CANINE FRIENDS

Perhaps the wisest and most serious dog on the acres was Sir General. In all his royalty, he was handsome and stately, with the looks belonging to a Golden Retriever and a Collie. His owners thought he was the best dog that there ever could be. They loved him so much that they actually fed him hamburgers and french fries as treats every so often. He guarded the property with great care and obeyed the owners' every command. For many years, he showered his owners with loyalty and love and was never, ever disobedient or unkind.

One stormy night, the owners were just about to close up the castle stable that housed most of their pets when Sir General began to bark and bark. His barking served as a warning signal that something was definitely amiss. The owners quickly went to the front door, and when they opened it, in with a huge gust of wind trotted the cutest black dog that they had ever seen.

Oh, my, thought General. *Look at her. Does she have any manners? And will she be a good house pet? And will she be kind and obedient like I am? And will she be polite?* worried the serious Sir General. *And, look at my owners. They think she is wonderful, and they don't even know anything about her.*

Oh, my, thought the new little black dog. *That beautiful orange dog is so big and so stern looking. I hope he likes me just a little bit. I am so lost, so I hope everyone here will like me and keep me forever, and, oh, my! Look at this beautiful home—I would love to stay here forever,* thought the little black dog with no name.

The Castle Hill Acres' owners were, of course, unaware of the dogs' thoughts but were so taken with the new addition that they embraced her with much love and sat down to think of a name for the new family member. Since she had white tips on all her toes, they decided to name her Miss Tippi, and, indeed, she seemed to dance on the tips of her toes every time they said how beautiful she was.

In the meantime, Sir General was not too pleased that his owners were acting so impulsively. *First of all,* he thought, *what if she is sick or bites or is unkind to all the other animals here?* He wondered, *What if they like her more than they like me? What if she does destructive things and I get blamed for them? What if they just stop loving me?* Poor General was so very sad and all of a sudden so very lonely. He unhappily went to bed for the rest of that stormy night and listened with a cocked ear to all the exciting banter about how wonderful this new little Tippi, who seemed to drop from heaven, was.

The next day, the bright reddish sun made its spectacular appearance as it usually did during the warm summer months. With it came the applause for Miss Tippi that Sir General knew was coming. The parents introduced her to all the members of the castle stable, and they all fell instantly in love with her, much to Sir General's chagrin. Although he smiled at his owners and he was obedient the whole day long, they still seemed to care for Miss Tippi more than for him. He was so distraught that he avoided being near Tippi, and every time that she came to him to be friends, he walked away.

Now, he thought, *I am being so impolite. I know that is not acceptable on the acres. Am I jealous? I must be, and I don't ever want to be mean or ignorant. I need to love her just as everyone else does,* he thought.

His owners, in the meantime, were so worried about how he was reacting to the new household member that they had started giving him lots of extra attention and treats. Sir General, in turn, felt even guiltier for being jealous, so he just curled up in a ball and fell fast asleep.

Oh, my, thought Tippi, *my new brother is so upset and unhappy. What should I do to show him how much I love him?* she pondered. *I need him to love me, too,* she thought. With that, she curled up and fell fast asleep.

That evening, another terrible thunderstorm erupted. This time, however, Tippi had gone outside to smell the flowers and was left in the storm. Oh, how frightened she was! She yipped and yelped and, pelted with hundreds of raindrops, she started to scratch at the main door. The owners opened the front door to find a dripping wet black mess of a dog. Sir General immediately, because he was like a guardian angel, began to lick the sweet little dog. He dried her as much as he could and then, in a gesture of pure love, placed his right paw around her little head, and they both dreamed of biscuits and hugs for the rest of the night.

Sir General was so excited when he awoke the next morning, for he was going to show his new companion the "ropes," so to speak. After a delicious breakfast of kibble and egg, he and Miss Tippi took a tour of the three-story brick house and the surrounding ten acres. He also explained, in great detail, how she should act as a good and somewhat perfect dog.

"Now, Tippi, you must obey all the rules, such as never jumping on the furniture, chasing the cats, or yipping at the horses' heels. Also," he added, "be sure to kiss your owners often, eat what is put in front of you, and never have an accident

in the house. By obeying and remaining a loyal, loving dog, you will be rewarded immensely."

After a few moments, as Miss Tippi was digesting all of the rules and regulations, Sir General added, "And, whatever you do, don't ever run away. Even if you see a rabbit bouncing through the hay field, and you think it wants to play hide and seek, forget it! That is one rule you must absolutely obey for as long as you live here."

"But," Miss Tippi responded, "I love to sprint and do one-mile dashes. It keeps me fit and trim and beautiful. What if I only did it for exercise?" she mused.

"Never," yelled the exasperated, orange dog. "I have lived here for eleven years, and of all the rules that must be kept, I know that is the most sacred."

Feeling a bit blue, Miss Tippi decided to lie down in the lush green grass to take a nap and dream of the days when she would run and run for miles and miles. Sir General, in the meantime, knew that she was unhappy; however, he also knew that Tippi would love living on the acres as much as every other animal did, so he never expected what would happen next.

A few months later, when the crispness of fall decorated the air, Sir General was taking one of his many naps in the late afternoon sun. Miss Tippi, who had long since settled into a daily routine that included watching the meadows while Sir General slept, was wistfully dreaming about the times when she would run and romp through the fields. Suddenly, out of nowhere, a considerable distance from the front meadow, Miss Tippi spied a beautiful deer, whose white tail glistened in the late afternoon sun. At once, she stood up, and being careful not to disturb Sir General, she tiptoed to the edge of the meadow. Forgetting the cardinal rule of obedience, Miss Tippi bolted full force through the field to meet the doe. Unfortunately, as luck would have it, the doe was more frightened than anything and ran with all her might through the neighboring forest.

Oh, my, thought Miss Tippi, *where did she go in such a hurry? I really want to meet her!* And with that, off she flew, the fastest dog in the universe at that moment. Because she was so excited, she didn't even realize that she had run into the dark forest and that the sun would soon be setting. For a few hours, she sniffed the doe's trail and ran along every path she could find, but Miss Tippi could still not find the friend she longed for. At long last, she decided that she had better return home before she got into more trouble. The problem, however, was that she was lost and had no inkling of which direction she should run.

In the meantime, back at Castle Hill Acres, Sir General began searching for his energetic black sidekick. Finally, after looking for an hour, he asked King Flash where she might be.

"Well, General," spoke King Flash thoughtfully, "I last saw her romping through the meadow trying to call a deer to her side. I whinnied and stomped, but she refused to listen," he added in his strong, deep voice.

It was now dark and quite cold for the season. To make matters worse, the night was cloudy and looked a bit stormy. Sir General, however, knew what he had to do, and he knew he had to do it quickly. After taking a long drink of water, the old dog began his trek to find the youngster.

The forest was even colder for Miss Tippi. More frightening yet were the strange noises. It wasn't long before she began to cry, "Somebody, please help me!" The only response Miss Tippi received was more screeching from the owls and howling from the now bitter cold wind. She thought—no, she actually believed that she would surely die underneath the giant swaying trees. Soon, gentle snow began to fall, and although it was beautiful, Miss Tippi was even more afraid that she'd die from frostbite. "Oh, why did I disobey? Now I will never get back to my wonderful home and family and food and water," cried the miserable Tippi.

Shivering from the unusual freeze, but determined to find his companion, Sir General trudged through the forest walls hoping to, at the very least, hear a sound that Miss Tippi might make. On and on for hours, the old dog made his feeble way, following every path and winding turn till at last he lay down to rest.

"A loyal dog never gives up," he sighed. "I must continue until I find her." With that, he hoisted his weary bones and rounded yet another bend in the sudden white blanket that covered the forest floor. Suddenly he heard a soft cry, and running towards a mound of white, General soon found a shivering, wet Tippi, who could barely say hello.

"Oh, Tippi," cried Sir General, "please get up—please don't die." Miss Tippi did not respond. Again Sir General pleaded for her to stand up, but she didn't budge. Instead, she just laid her head down on the forest floor and stared straight ahead. General did the only thing he knew to do and that was to cover her body with his. The snowflakes soon covered Sir General, but he knew that he was saving Miss Tippi's life, so he just kept dreaming about his bed in front of the cozy fireplace at home.

Around daybreak, Miss Tippi struggled to rise, but Sir General was just too tired and cold. "Oh, General," she wailed, "I am so sorry that I disobeyed and made you so sick. Please wake up. Please take me home. Please don't die." Tippi now did the only thing she knew to do and that was to lick General's gentle face until he would awaken. Gradually, the old dog stirred, and with a yelp of excitement, Miss Tippi scrambled out from under him. Sir General, although very weary, soon mustered enough strength to stand and nuzzle sweet Tippi.

With that, the serious dog and the playful pup began their journey back to Castle Hill Acres, where love, food, and warmth awaited them. For a few years after that, Miss Tippi took care of Sir General until the day he died, and she remained a loyal and obedient dog who appreciated all the gifts she had found that one stormy night years before.

THE DOG WHO QUACKED

Whenever someone new came to live at Castle Hill Acres, King Flash would always offer much needed advice to the wayward, and he would often relate heartwarming stories about Master Bernie and how he loved everyone despite their differences.

"This is one of the most important lessons you will ever learn here," advised King Flash very seriously. "Always love everyone no matter how different from you they may be." And so, the newcomer, whether it was a fluffy kitten, a field mouse, a tiny sparrow, an energetic colt, a lost puppy, or a grumpy groundhog, listened to the "Bernie" stories. When King Flash spoke, all listened. He often reminded them that in order to remain at Castle Hill Acres, all the creatures must try to act like their hero, Master Bernie.

Although he sported beautiful tan and white feathery fur, was the perfect size—not terribly big or small—performed his tasks as a hunting dog in the best way possible, and was loyal, Master Bernie's best trait was that he was compassionate. He often told King Flash that he only hunted with his owner because he wanted to be obedient. Truthfully, it made the poor dog quite sad every time a pheasant was shot for dinner. On those particular nights, he would actually cry himself to sleep.

It was no surprise, therefore, that Master Bernie liked to live outside in a dog box so that he could be the first to help any lost or injured creature on the acres. He soon became known as the resident nurse, doctor, psychiatrist, and babysitter. Most, however, liked the kindly dog because he was a friend to all and accepted their differences with love and understanding.

One time, for instance, he helped the groundhogs by digging holes for them so that they would have a comfortable home for the winter.

Yet another time, the owners discovered him in the house sleeping in front of the fireplace beside two cats and a lonely brown mouse. Still another time, he nursed an injured bird back to life.

One damp and foggy grey morning, Master Bernie had just finished his breakfast when he saw two snowy white ducks with bright orange beaks waddle towards his dog box.

"Excuse me, sir," said the female duck, with a worried look in her eye. "We are so lost and cannot find the stream. Would you please help us?" Master Bernie was delighted to have their company, and it just so happened that the clearest blue stream around ran right behind his box, so he took them there immediately.

"Chloe is going to have a family, so we could not waddle around all day trying to find a suitable spot," the male duck Casper added.

"I am ever so pleased to help you both," softly barked Bernie. "Just be careful that the wild dog across the way doesn't harm your pretty white feathers. He is quite mean, so please stay away from him. I will also keep watch for you."

For many days and weeks, pretty little Chloe sat on her nest in between short swims and lunches with their new friend Bernie. Casper, her mate, would often bring home special treats for all of them, and they would tell each other stories about the old days. Of course, Master Bernie loved their company, and he especially liked helping them. Napping with them was the highlight of his days. He often imitated them, too, in an effort to make them feel comfortable in their new surroundings.

"Why must he shake his body as if he has tail feathers?" criticized the barn animals.

"Why, he is acting ridiculous, if you ask me," scoffed Sir Alex.

King Flash often had to quell any criticism by emphatically stating, "Don't criticize Master Bernie for being so kind; he's making a big difference around here by accepting others just the way they are. And don't forget that being unique brings color to this world of ours," stated wise King Flash. "And furthermore, we are not put on this earth to judge, but to love." With that, he stomped emphatically.

One misty morning, Master Bernie awakened to a terrible sound—the snarling of the mean grey dog from across the stream. With a mad dash, Master Bernie jumped across the stream to find his friend Casper lying weakly by the water's edge.

"Oh, Casper," Bernie cried, "let me help you."

"It's too late," replied the dying duck. "I was protecting my dear, sweet Chloe from him. He was going to hurt her and the eggs." With great effort, he gasped, "I did what I had to do." With that, Casper lay lifeless.

In the meantime, Chloe was hysterical, and poor Master Bernie could not seem to calm her.

"Oh, Chloe, I will take care of you. I promise to be the best friend you have ever had," he wept. "I will do anything just to make you happy and smile again," he added.

Unfortunately, Chloe was far too upset and lamely hobbled over to the edge of the stream bank and wept and wept. For days and days, Master Bernie sat with her, brought her nourishment, and kept her warm. Chloe never did return to her nest, so Bernie would keep the eggs warm for her.

"Oh, King Flash," cried Princess Flower, "what is poor Bernie doing? He hardly eats, and he's acting like a duck of all things," she wailed.

"Well, my little Flower, Master Bernie is giving himself to someone else so that she will be happier some day. What he is doing is very selfless. Our world would be so much better if we all acted like him," mused the black and white steed.

One beautiful, yellow April day, the huge sun shone brighter than ever, the red and orange flowers swayed proudly in the gentle breeze, and the day promised to be filled with joy. On this particular day, Master Bernie was lying on the nest when he felt something strange happen beneath him.

"Oh, Chloe," he excitedly barked, "please come here quickly. Something is happening, and I don't know what to do next."

With that, the dejected duck waddled over to her nest, only to discover that her three eggs were hatching! "Oh, my," she loudly quacked. "Oh, my! Bernie, we're having babies!" she said with a louder quack. One by one, each of the babies poked through their filmy shell and squinted in the bright sunlight. And one by one, they all made their way to their mother Chloe who, with tears of joy, nudged and hugged them until they fell asleep.

"My dearest friend, Bernie," she sobbed, "how can I thank you enough for all that you have done. I now have a reason to wake up every morning with a smile on my face," she tearfully added.

For years after that, Master Bernie watched the babies grow and even helped them to waddle and quack properly. Most of all, however, he protected and loved them as if they were his own and every once in a while, he would pretend to shake the tail feathers he did not have.

PEPPER GETS A SECOND CHANCE

I was totally stranded; I had absolutely no idea where I was, how I got there, or where I was heading. To make matters worse, I was starving, thirsty, and exhausted. I also felt really sick. Actually, I was too weak to keep going, so I was really happy when some nice people called me over from the middle of the highway and offered me some water and crackers. Little did they know that their lives would be forever transformed with me in their stately abode.

Now, I must also mention that I was not the most handsome boy on the block. My jaws sagged, my legs were long and gangly, I slobbered, and my black and white spots were endless. They kind of meshed into one grayish blob. The only distinguishing features that caught everyone's attention were my long, and I mean long, black ears. At least I had some things going for me.

It wasn't long before my new owners knew I would be trouble. First of all, I stepped all over my new "mother," and her brand new white slacks were covered with grease and oil. Next, I couldn't help myself—I was so excited—so I had an accident in the car. Finally, I would not stand still. Thank goodness they owned a van because I needed room to release all of my excitable energy.

At long last, we arrived at the very impressive Castle Hill Acres. Of the many animals there, one shaggy grey and white dog bounced around the corner and cautiously greeted me. *Where are his eyes?* I thought. Later I learned that he was an Old English Sheepdog, so he always had hidden eyes. That made me a little nervous, not being able to see the whites of his eyes and all that. To make matters worse, he had a strange accent when he spoke to me.

"I say, bloke," critically stated Sir Alex, "who are you, and are you really a dog or a Martian?"

"Hey, dude," I replied, "glad to make your acquaintance and all that. I'm digging my new pad," I said, trying to be cool.

"We'll see how long our family puts up with the likes of you," responded Sir Alex, somewhat put off by this new member's slang. After all, one must remember that Sir Alex was quite a distinguished Britisher.

The next thing I knew, my new owners put me in a bubble bath, of all things. They scrubbed and scrubbed until I couldn't stand myself anymore. Then this awful noisy contraption blew hot air all over me until I thought I would just die! The results, however, certainly outweighed the miserable moments, for my new owners could not stop hugging and kissing me. I, in turn, was so excited that I had another accident. Who could blame me, though, because the carpet was as green as a meadow during Spring. Needless to say, Sir Alex had something to say about that.

"Whatever were you thinking, or don't you think at all?" he barked. "I can see this will not be a pleasant house with you in it."

"I beg your highness's pardon," I retorted. "Haven't you ever had accidents and stuff? You can't be that perfect."

"Oh, believe me. Misbehavior and disrespect are not very welcome on these premises," Sir Alex added. "If you are not careful, you might just find yourself playing on the highway again. All of the other animals here are lovable, intelligent, considerate, and obedient. I do not suggest that you deviate from this type of behavior."

"Yo, dude, you are such a snob," I barked. Immediately I was sorry I had said this. I knew I needed a friend and that kind of response didn't make anything but enemies.

In the meantime, the new owners decided to name me Pepper. I felt I was more regal than that goofy name. I would have preferred Maximillian, or Nicholas, or Baxter, but at the moment, I was already in trouble the first night there, so I decided to reluctantly go along with the less desirable name.

After a beautiful night's rest in the owners' four-poster bed, I was whisked off to the veterinarian's office for a full workup. Wow! It was so much fun greeting everyone else, jumping on the receptionist's counter, and bopping all the pet owners with my big tail. One lady even limped away after I knocked her into the wall. The owners were mortified. The vet, however, thought I was the coolest dog he had ever seen. From that day on, he was my buddy. After shots and deworming, I headed back to the acres for more fun and games.

Flower gardens have always interested me, especially the ones with deep, dark mulch. You never know what you might find buried in there. Sure enough, I found one on the acres' property. I never knew I could have so much fun! I even picked some flowers off the ground to give to my new owners. My "mother" screamed and cried that I had ruined something. Actually, it really looked better than it had before.

"Here it is only day two," lectured Sir Alex, "and already you have destroyed property and upset the two people in the world who truly love you. What is wrong with you?"

"I don't have anything wrong with me, dude," I snapped. "Why don't you have some fun around here? It might help you lighten up."

With that, I strolled into the house and plopped my gangly and, I will admit, somewhat dirty body on the new white sofa. Unfortunately, when I slept, I also slobbered. The owners did their best to scrub the slobber, but after a few months, the consensus remained that a new sofa needed to be purchased. The owners, devoted to their usually wonderful animals, took this all in stride, saying that they hoped I would become a more civilized member of the household. Time, however, let them know that this was not going to happen. Even Sir Alex gave up helping me to improve. "The dog is hopeless," he stated.

For months, I still believed that the green carpet was grass, that the potted Christmas tree was an outside fire hydrant, and that I could do whatever I pleased whenever I wished. Even ripping a piece of aluminum siding from the house was a big game for me. Things were ruined, the house was in an uproar, and the other animals complained every day about me.

But I didn't mind because I was having so much fun, and the food here was so delicious.

"He'll never become Sir Pepper," bellowed King Flash. "The boy is incorrigible."

"I say," remarked Sir Alex, "he is driving me crazy. He's a hooligan."

"He's so sloppy," meowed Princess Flower. "He shakes his body, and slobber flies everywhere."

"And," piped up Pokey, "he tossed a lot of stones and dirt into the pool the other day, and he even had the nerve to say that he didn't care since he didn't have to clean it up."

"Worse yet," cried Prince Smitty, "he doesn't stay clean and runs through the house, making everything dirty. I don't know why our owners put up with him."

"It's probably because they love so deeply," said King Flash, in deep thought. "Perhaps, we should give Pepper another chance or two. Just maybe he will begin to understand how a dog should act here at Castle Hill Acres," he stated with a shake of his black mane. He added, "After dinner, bring him to me, Sir Alex. It's time for a little chat."

After a beautiful meal of kibble and leftover steak bones, Sir Alex told me to meet him in the stables. Since I wanted to play instead, I chased four kittens until they screeched for their mom. Then I decided to eat all of their food in the stable area. I was never as frightened as I was when I stepped inside. There, pawing and snorting was the biggest animal I had ever seen close up. His name read "King Flash." I thought that was interesting since he didn't have a crown on his head. Fortunately for me, he was behind stall bars.

"Pepper," he seemed to growl, "who do you think you are around here?"

"Why, I am the king of the hill, the cool dude from nowhere, and I have it made in the shade, bro," responded the discourteous dog.

"Let me tell you something, young man," King Flash snarled in exasperation. "You don't seem to understand the concept of unconditional love. Those who receive it should, at the very least, try to be kind and good in return. Have you even seen the owners smile at you lately?

Yet they continue to shower you with all kinds of love and--"

"Listen, big bro," I interrupted, "I don't care, and anyway, what are you going to do about it? You're locked in a cage. I'd say that you're the one around here who needs to learn some kind of a lesson. I'm not penned up." With that, I turned around and decided to stroll through the meadow.

I thought I was hot stuff. Here I had this thing called unconditional love and all the comforts of a wonderful home. Better yet, despite my memory lapses that made me do some fairly destructive acts, I still had a good home. What did that so-called king know anyway?

"Hey, you," yelled some men in blue jumpsuits with shiny badges.

"Are you hollering at me?" I barked in reply.

Suddenly, a huge, white net covered me and I realized I was in serious trouble. How I longed for a bubble bath right about now. Before long, I found my tall body stuck in a tiny metal cage with many miserable dogs surrounding me. *So much for moving around,* I thought. The other dogs in the "society"—I thought it was a club—were crying to me that their owners weren't coming to get them, so they were going to die.

"Yo, dudes," I panicked. "Enough of the horror stories! Your owners love you unconditionally, don't they?" By this time, I felt a sick knot about to strangle my insides. What if they were right?

For days, I suffered heartache. One by one, I watched as some owners came for their lost dogs, while others were taken to another room. Where could my owners be? Maybe they didn't love me anymore. After all, being as selfish as I was certainly didn't make them happy. I also could not stop thinking about what the king had said. *Oh,* I thought, *I don't want to die. If only I could have another chance.*

Rain clouds, thick and black, ushered in the dawn of the next day. Dogs were howling, cats were meowing, and a man in a black sweater came to let me out of the cage. Shaking like a leaf on a stormy day, I slowly walked my way towards the "room." All of a sudden, I smelled someone familiar. I pulled and pulled on the leash and planted my four skinny black and white feet on the concrete. "Could it be? Could it be my owners?" With that, in ran my owners who were crying and happy all at the same time. I, in turn, not wanting to misbehave again, just stood there.

"Isn't he happy to see us?" questioned my "mom." Oh, but I was, and with that, I bounded into her arms and proceeded to slobber her with kisses. She, of course, didn't seem to mind, even when she had to pay to take me away.

For the rest of the day, I played nicely with the kittens, I apologized to King Flash, I stayed off the sofa and out of the flower beds, and I even shared my food with Sir Alex. I also obeyed all the rules. It felt so good to put my head on my pillow that night in my owners' bed and know that I was still loved, and that most importantly, I had finally done something right. I am to this day known only as Pepper, but perhaps in a few years, the rest of the animals will dub me with knighthood or maybe even make me a prince.

LOLA DISCOVERS REAL DAZZLE

During one extremely cold and long winter in Pennsylvania, snow blanketed the ground for months. Gray days stretched into still gloomier ones, and all of the animals were sad and sluggish.

"Oh, King Flash," Princess Flower cried, as she shivered from the cold, "it's freezing. I feel like all I do is sleep in the hay. When will the weather get better?"

"Well, Flower," King Flash replied, "all any of us can do is try to stay warm and dream of sunny, hot days. We could all use some excitement around here, though," he thoughtfully added.

As fate would have it, a visitor brought the gloomy residents exactly what they wished for and more. Who would ever forget Lola, the cousin from Europe? In all her finery, this pure white Standard Poodle pranced into Castle Hill Acres and let everyone know how important she was.

"Oh, my," she sneered, "why aren't you washed and brushed perfectly like I am? Why is your right ear black and the other one white? You have a very big nose as well. And why is it sooo cold here? And where should I put my designer bowls and place mats?"

"Oh, brother," piped in Sir Oliver, the resident Old English Sheepdog, who would be attending the very same dog show as Lola would. Now we must mention that his name, Rollickin's Little Dickens, was a perfect fit for this clown of a dog who loved to play and stir up trouble. He also was perhaps the kindest dog anyone could want to know.

"Don't be so rude, dog," Lola quipped. The last I looked, you were wearing a shabby collar. Look at mine; it has diamonds and is the finest pink collar available and — it is made by Poochie, the famous designer. At least everyone will like me because I have nothing but the finest in attire and accessories. Even my brushes are designed especially for me. See, they have my name on them."

"Whatever," laughed Sir Oliver. "Somehow, though, I didn't hear that wearing and owning designer wear would make you more important than someone else. Come with me; I want you to meet the 'head of the household,' so to speak." With that, he whisked her into the stable area where she proceeded to cough, shiver, and whine.

"What is this ghastly place? Doesn't anyone vacuum in here ever? Who are all those creatures, especially the tall black and white one?"

"Why, Lola, my name is King Flash. I am so pleased to meet you, finally. We have all heard much about how well you do on the show circuit and, of course, how beautiful you are."

"Not that I am pleased to meet you, but, yes, I am beautiful, don't you think?"

King Flash began to snicker, and with a stomp of his hoof, told her that she would need to change her ways if she were going to stay for any length of time at the acres. With that, Lola, in all her supposed glory, turned on her perfectly

manicured toenails, and with her snowy white head held high, she sashayed out of the barn.

The very next day, the sun shone brightly through the lattice windowpanes, the little brown birds were chirping excitedly, and the weatherman was promising a much warmer day. Lola, however, was not in the least bit happy about the day or her company. She was forced to eat the other dogs' boring food (they didn't get chicken or steak), and her designer bowls were nowhere to be found. To top it all off, Sir Oliver was racing through the mansion and was tracking mud wherever he went. This proved to be too much for Lola, who found a spot out of his path and carefully licked her paws to "get the germs off."

Show time was fast approaching and every animal on the acres was excited to see who would win Best in Show. Pokey, of course, rooted for Sir Oliver, as did all the other residents. Unfortunately, Lola had annoyed everyone so much that they found it difficult to even compliment her. In the meantime, Lola was practicing her show walk throughout the house, while Sir Oliver went to King Flash for evaluation.

"Keep your head high, young man, and be careful not to seem nervous. Your walk is fluid and good. Just make sure that you pay careful attention to everything the handler tells you to do, but most importantly," King Flash added, "make sure that you smile and maintain your very friendly personality. The judges like that a lot. I know that when I was on the show circuit, the judges liked how I acted and not necessarily how perfect my mane was. I know you will do very well. Now, go and get your bath and stand still for your grooming appointment," King Flash pronounced. "You are the man of the hour," the king boasted.

Even though it was another cold, windy, gray day, the dog show seemed to be alive with warmth and sunshine. Owners were fussing over their beautiful dogs, and the handlers were making last-minute preparations before the judging began.

"Aren't you nervous that you will be eliminated during the first round?" Lola asked Sir Oliver as she pranced in a circle. "Why, just look at me! How do you like my designer wear and new coat whitener?"

"You look great," Oliver replied as he jumped excitedly from the grooming table. "How do I look? All that grooming is sure a hassle." Sir Oliver beamed.

"Well, let's put it this way," Lola replied with a haughty look, "you could look a bit more dignified instead of acting like such a clown. And whose idea was it to comb your shaggy hair like that?"

Oliver hung his head with those remarks and forced himself to hear King Flash's encouraging words. *He was so proud of me,* Sir Oliver thought.

As the show progressed, the preliminary champions were carefully chosen, based on their movement, appearance, and personality. It was, therefore, no surprise that Sir Oliver won his herding class and that Lola managed a victory in the nonsporting dog category. The finals would be a battle to the finish, as all the dogs selected for Best in Breed coveted the Best in Show trophy. The announcers, it seemed, also had their favorites as the top finishers entered the giant show ring.

"Just look at that beautiful Poodle—Lola, I believe. She certainly is impressive, and check out the collar! But she seems a bit unfriendly and detached. Her handler seems to sense it. Hopefully, she can show a bit more dazzle."

"Why, would you just look at Rollickin's Little Dickens, or Oliver, as he is affectionately named. He is absolutely stealing the hearts of everyone here. Just look at that smile. He certainly seems to be happy. And, can he move! The judge seems to be enjoying him as well," excitedly added another announcer.

"Larry, this will certainly be a tough call today. These dogs are all spectacular in their own way. Oh, the judge is taking some aside. Will you look at that! She has pulled Oliver and three others. She told the others to go around one more time. Well, I think she has made up her mind," the announcer excitedly shouted.

"Well, Mike, you called it. She's chosen Oliver. Just look at how excited he seems to be. It always amazes me how these dogs know when they have won. The surprise of the day, though, is that the foreign champion, Lola, did not even place."

On the long journey to Castle Hill, Lola cried and cried. She tearfully stated, "I am ruined. No one will ever love me again."

Sir Oliver felt so sorry for her that he wished she had won instead. "Oh, Lola," he compassionately said, "everyone will still love you. You don't need ribbons or trophies or special stuff to make you loved. You only need to be yourself and love others, too."

For days after the show, poor Lola refused to eat. She kept saying how she did not know what was to become of her since she was such a loser. Finally, Sir Oliver convinced her to visit the wise and wonderful King Flash once again.

"Oh, Lola, Lola, Lola, you are such a treasure just being a dog," King Flash gently whinnied. "You need to understand that possessions and prizes are only fleeting—they disappear eventually—and they certainly don't make you a better dog. Please promise me that you will try to greet other people in a friendly manner, and maybe you will feel a lot better about who you are as the dog God created." With that, Big King Flash rubbed his coal black muzzle against her pure white head. Lola had never felt so much love and acceptance than in that very moment.

With the help of most of the animals, Lola visited the neighbors, wagged her tail often, began to romp with the others, and actually snuggled with the owners. She even dreamed sweet dreams of people hugging and loving her without her expensive things.

Because she realized that the designer fashions did not make her a better dog and that she was actually loved more when she focused on loving others, Lola decided to bury her expensive collars and bowls, brushes, and combs. "I don't need those things to feel good anymore," she proudly barked to King Flash.

The best part of all was the party that the animal residents threw for Lola. Complete with chicken, pink party hats, carrot cake and vanilla ice cream, the party was the happiest time she had ever had. Her biggest surprise, however, was the banner that Sir Oliver presented to her which read, "Best in Show—for realizing that true beauty and worth lie within you."

INDAY TAKES THE WRONG LEAD

Quite often, on one of the lush green hills of Castle Hill Acres, one could observe the frolicking of two very beautiful colts, Princess Inday and Prince Reron. To the observer, the grey and white filly, sporting a thick, beautiful steel gray mane and tail, seemed to always be in charge of the handsome, sleek and slender, chestnut colt, Prince Reron, who, more often than not, followed her everywhere.

"Oh, Reron," squealed Inday with delight as she chased after the two resident wool-bearers, Heidi and Abigail. "Hurry up! This is so much fun. See how they Baa and fly through the air when you run after them."

"No," Reron whinnied, "my mom told me never to make others feel uncomfortable, and at this very moment, you are frightening them. Please stop chasing them," Prince Reron cried as the two sheep bleated their dissatisfaction over the entire ordeal.

The truth was that Princess Inday, with her huge white blaze and the most beautiful brown eyes in the horse world, loved to tease other animals, and, most importantly, loved to let Prince Reron, the promising contender in a Kentucky Derby race, know that she was fearless. As far as she was concerned, her behavior was "cute." Prince Reron, on the other hand, did fear her recklessness and seemed to know better than anyone (except for King Flash) that her behavior would surely lead to trouble someday.

"Inday," he snorted, "please leave them alone." No sooner did he utter his plea when, all of a sudden, the wooly masses dove through the fence and landed in the blue stream. Princess Inday was so amused that she just stood by the fence and giggled until she heard her mother, Lindee, who was snorting her disapproval.

"Inday," she hollered, "just because you were born on July 4, does not give you license to be

independent of the rules around here! Now, gallop yourself right back into the stables, and stay there while I help these poor ewes."

"Oh, Mom," Princess Inday responded, shaking her long mane, "I was just having some fun around here. Haven't you ever gotten bored with life here on the acres?"

"That will be quite enough, young lady. Now do as I say without another word, or there will be no extra hay for you this evening," the massive grey mare exclaimed.

Reluctantly, Princess Inday trotted back to her stall, only to find the young prince laughing at her.

"Ha, I told you not to scare them. I bet you'll be grounded forever now," he said with a toss of his silky, chestnut mane.

"Reron," she replied, "you are much too serious for someone your age. There will be plenty of time for you to follow the rules when you are on the race track. Furthermore, I don't appreciate your criticism. Let's just have some fun around here for a change." With that, she pranced into her stall and munched on a juicy red apple.

Of course, no one could possibly know what the mischievous Inday would do next. The very next day, as Prince Reron was practicing his sprints through the pasture, he noticed that the naughty princess was trying to jump the fence.

"Come on, Reron," she urged, "let's see if we can cross over to that meadow with the bright yellow flowers. We'll surely have a lot of fun," she nickered.

"Oh, Inday," Prince Reron protested, "I don't think it's a very good idea to either a) jump the fence or b) graze in that meadow. Our moms never told us we could do that."

"Oh, you are such a scaredy-cat, Reron," yelled Princess Inday. With that, she ran with all her might and just barely made it to the other side.

"See?" she asked. "No problem. Now, you do it, too."

Prince Reron, not wanting to look foolish or let a girl beat him at anything, ran back as far as he could with all his sprinting might, and, with a leap, he tried to clear the fence, but his young back legs hit, and Reron landed in a heap.

"Oh," he cried, "help me, Inday. Go get my mom. I'm really hurt."

"I bet you're not," the filly yelled. She was, however, quite frightened that his racing career might be over.

Later that evening, while the vet was helping Prince Reron, Lindee and Reron's mom, Gala, decided that Princess Inday needed more guidance.

"Inday," stated elegant Gala, in her usual prim and proper voice, "what you did today could most definitely have resulted in a tragedy of the most serious kind. My young colt has the makings of a true winner on the race track. How would you feel if he had broken a leg and would have to be put down? Better yet, how would you be able to live with that guilt for the rest of your life, knowing that you encouraged him to do something so dangerous?"

"Indeed," added Lindee, "your behavior today is highly unacceptable, young lady. And even though Reron should not have followed your foolish behavior, you still set an extremely poor example. You will be separated for quite some time now; Reron has to heal, and you need to think about your bad behavior."

And so, for months, the two beautiful colts remained far apart from one another. Prince Reron grew gracefully and healed perfectly and began practicing for the Kentucky Derby time trials, while Princess Inday went to horse shows and created all kinds of problems. For instance, as a yearling in the halter class, she saw something of great interest outside the show ring and decided that jumping up to see it was acceptable behavior. Needless to say, she did not win any ribbons in that class and proceeded to distract everyone around her. Her mother just shook her long silver mane, as she was unsure of what to do next.

"Oh, King Flash," cried Lindee, "what should I do? She never listens, and all she wants to do is have fun the wrong way," she sobbed.

"My dear," stated King Flash, "she is a good girl, but she will learn the hard way, I suspect. Some children are like that. All we can hope for is that it won't be a tragic lesson," he stated as he shook his thick, black mane. "Peer pressure is tough," he added with a snort.

After a few months, the two yearlings were once again allowed to play together, and, although they did not romp and frolic as they used to as yearlings, they still enjoyed a good laugh together and the companionship of having a best friend. Princess Inday remained the perfect lady and did not encourage Prince Reron to follow her lead in any crazy schemes... except for one day, a week before Reron's Kentucky Derby time trial.

As chance would have it, the groundskeeper accidentally left the gate open that led to the pear tree pasture. Even though their moms had told them repeatedly to never venture out of their designated pasture, Princess Inday could not help exploring.

"Come on, Reron," she excitedly whinnied, "I bet those pears taste sooo good, and I am soooo hungry." With that, she trotted toward the trees with Prince Reron close on her heels.

"I'm not so sure we should eat any pears," he exclaimed. "We might get sick."

"Oh, silly," chimed Inday, "apples don't hurt us, so why should pears? Besides, you need to keep your strength up for next week. Someone as strong and athletic as you should not be worrying over whether a pear will make you sick. Look, I'll eat the first one."

So, with another bat of her beautiful dark eyelashes, Princess Inday devoured the prettiest green and red pear on the tree. Prince Reron, not to be outshone, did the same. The only problem was that neither colt stopped with just one. Soon, many, many, many delicious pears were eaten before someone realized that the colts were in the pear tree pasture.

Later that evening, rain and wind descended on Castle Hill Acres like never before. The lights flickered on and off, and all of the animals were restless. King Flash paced in his stall, Prince Smitty hid behind a hay bale, and Pokey the possum was too frightened to eat. Matrons Lindee and Gala were just about ready to tuck their little ones in for the night when Prince Reron started to perspire and roll. This was indeed a very bad sign, for it indicated that he had a bad bellyache. In the horse world, this meant that he could die. Gala began to kick her stall with all her sixteen-hand might, which alerted the owners.

Within minutes, the vet arrived and determined that the young prince was very sick. He then received several shots, and the vet inserted a tube through Prince Reron's nose that extended into his belly. The vet then pumped gallons of mineral oil into Prince Reron's belly to help him recover. It was at this point that the vet informed the owners that he was not sure that the Kentucky Derby hopeful would make it. Throughout the night, the owners had to administer shots and walk the colt in the hopes that he would heal.

"Oh, Reron," Inday cried, "please get better. What a stupid thing I have done! I am so sorry that I don't think before I do things," she stomped and cried.

"Inday," responded a very worried Gala, "Reron did not have to eat those pears. Just because you suggested it did not mean that he had to eat them. As usual, he had a choice to make, and it happened to be the wrong one. You should feel terrible for influencing him the way you did, but he should have used more common sense," she said tearfully.

All through the dark and stormy night, Prince Reron struggled and suffered. The next morning when the vet returned, he was not much better. It was then that Princess Inday heard the dreaded words, "We should consider putting him down." After another dose of mineral oil, the vet decided that if Reron did not improve in a few hours, he would return to euthanize him.

"Oh, Reron," sobbed Inday, "please get better. I promise I will never ever lead you in the wrong direction. You are my best friend, and I just don't know what I would do without you! Start thinking about how you are going to win the race of your life. I know you can do it," she added with a swish of her thick tail.

Many long hours passed; the owners and all the other animals prayed and cried. All of a sudden, as if he were racing out of the starting gate, Prince Reron whinnied and cried that he felt better. The animals raced around cheering, and at the sound of their excitement, Reron jumped up and shouted, "Give me some hay, please!" Princess Inday had never in her short life ever heard words as beautiful as those. With a snort, they nuzzled each other and from that moment on, their lives were changed forever.

Much to everyone's surprise, especially her mother's, Princess Inday was a top show horse who actually placed first in a nationally ranked show. She was as stately as her dam and as showy as her sire. Prince Reron went on to place second in the Kentucky Derby, first in the Preakness, and third in the Belmont Stakes. But, most importantly, both horses not only remained best friends, but they also taught their colts that doing what someone else wants you to do rather than what you are taught can lead to terrible consequences...as well as a tongue lashing by King Flash.

A LITTLE DOG SAVES A LIFE

Christmas time was always a festive occasion at Castle Hill Acres. The house and stable area were decorated with many twinkling white lights, wreathes glowed with red and gold sparkles, and the Christmas tree looked as if it belonged in the North Pole with its candy canes, gingerbread ornaments, and frosted mints. The animals, too, loved the excitement and looked forward to the special day when they would get a "love" gift—the extra-special kind from the owners. Each Christmas brought interesting visitors from the owners' families, and that, too, was always a treat to enjoy.

And so it was that on the Christmas Eve before the first big snowfall of King Flash's twenty-fifth year that a very small cousin, Little

Bro, more affectionately known as Yittle, came to stay at Castle Hill. Now, one must mention that Yittle was indeed very, very little. He was a white French Bulldog with extraordinarily big ears. The owners loved him very much, though, so they overlooked any imperfections. Yittle, on the other hand, was not really happy with himself. However, it was Christmas Eve, and he, too, could hardly wait for the special gift he would receive.

As was tradition, King Flash called an important meeting to wish the animals a very merry Christmas and to remind them that they should remember that the day is not about the gifts.

"Now, my wonderful friends, I want you to remember that this special day is about the love that you feel for each other. Don't forget that you should spread cheer and love, all year long, to those you meet. And, most importantly," he added with a huge swish of his gleaming black tail, "you should be happy with the gifts that God has given you and share them with others."

All of the animals were in awe of this beautiful steed, and they believed with all their hearts that what he said would guarantee them happiness. After all, he was the king. Yittle, although a bit afraid of this huge beast, smiled as he thought of the happy day ahead, but at the same time, he could not think of any special gift that he owned that he could share with others.

Soon, after many yawns, all the animals returned to their little beds and dreamed of the wonderful treats they would receive the next day. Yittle, however, dreamed of how he didn't fit in with the animals of Castle Hill Acres.

Sometimes when we think of all the wrong things about ourselves, we fail to see the absolutely wonderful things about us. This, unfortunately, for the little guest Yittle, was the case. Not only did he cry about how he did not fit in all night long, he felt as if he should never have been born. Poor Yittle; little did he know that he would one day sparkle more than any diamond in the entire world.

The next day, wrapping paper in all shades of red, green, blue, white, and silver, along with bright, colorful bows flew in all directions as the animals tore into their "love" gifts.

Even King Flash eagerly devoured his bowl of bran mash and carrots. Yittle, however, remained sullen in the corner of the Great Room, and he refused to enjoy the festivities.

"Oh, Sir General," whispered Princess Flower, "why is Yittle so sad?"

"I'm not so certain, sweet Flower, but I will try to find out. After all, he is a treasured member of the family, so someone should try to make him happy," stated Sir General in his very serious voice.

Sir Oliver also noticed the change in Yittle and asked him what the matter could be.

Yittle responded only with, "Nothing."

"Don't you like your new red ball?" asked Sir Oliver.

"I guess," responded Yittle. With that, he retreated into a corner of the darkened den and was not seen for many hours.

In the meantime, all of the animals, including the bat and rat, enjoyed their gifts and special food treats as the adults ate turkey, stuffing, and trimmings to conclude an incredible day.

Later that snowy evening, Yittle sat in a dark corner and cried his little heart out. It was then that Miss Tippi came to him and licked his tears away.

"Oh, Yittle," she cried, "whatever is the problem? Didn't you have a wonderful day as we did?"

"No, sobbed Yittle. "I am so unhappy, Miss Tippi. Do you want to know why?"

"Of course, I do, Yittle. Nobody should ever be unhappy here at the acres, especially on Christmas Day. There is too much love and forgiveness for that," she added with a bark.

"Well, first of all," he cried, "I am a freak! I am too short, I am fat, I snort like a pig, I have an unusual odor, and my ears are too big," he wailed.

Sir Alex could not help remarking, "I say, little chap, whatever are you talking about? I think you are rather cute in your own little way. Think of all the other hundreds of creatures in the universe that are plain unattractive," he affectionately stated with a wink of his eye. "Besides which," he added, "no one at the acres is ever anything but unique and perfect in their own way."

This, however, did nothing to make Yittle feel better. Instead of enjoying the warmth and glow of a beautiful holiday, he wanted to disappear into the gloom of unhappiness.

The stable animals were all aflutter, talking about their gifts—the best ever—and how they would share them with each other. Pokey decided that the perch he received so that he could swing upside down on it with his tail would also make a splendid scratching post for the kittens. The kittens, on the other hand, thought that their kitty condo would be great for Barry to snuggle in on cold nights. All in all, they went to sleep feeling as if they were the happiest animals in the world.

King Flash, however, paced all night, wondering how he could make the little visitor happy. He shared his concerns with Prince Smitty, who was too excited to sleep.

"Prince Smitty," he began, "did you talk to that cute little dog, Yittle?"

"Why, yes, I did briefly," replied the fat cat.

"What have you observed about him this fine evening?" asked the king.

"Well, sir, I know he feels as if he doesn't fit in, and I don't think he feels that he has any special gifts or talents," meowed Prince Smitty.

"This could be a serious problem," whispered King Flash. "Tomorrow, we need to talk to him. Now, go to sleep so you don't get sick," Flash added.

The next morning dawned with a bright yellow sun, with just a hint of a cold winter breeze in the air. After the animals ate their various breakfasts filled with assorted treats, King Flash, once again, called a meeting with Yittle as the guest of honor.

"It seems as though you are very unhappy with us, Little Yittle," whinnied the king. "Would you like to share your concerns with us?"

"Why, why, no, Mr. Flash," softly replied Yittle, "I'm not unhappy with you. It's just that I am not tall like Pepper, I don't have a lot of hair like Sir Alex, I don't have a soft, big nose like Sir Oliver, I don't swing from perches like Pokey, I don't purr like the kittens, I don't fly like a bat, I don't jump over fences like Princess Inday, and I am not handsome like you. I can't do anything but snort like a piglet," he sobbed.

"But, Yittle," King Flash responded as he stomped affectionately, "you have a gift that can be shared that is unique to you. You do not need to compare yourself to anyone else. Someday you will find that out, but in the meantime, you need to know that you are special, no matter what you think."

As each snowy day passed, Yittle became more and more depressed. The owners were so busy preparing for their New Year's Eve guests that they didn't even notice how much Yittle hid. As was customary, each new year was celebrated by bringing someone who was experiencing a hardship to the acres to spend two fun-filled days with the family. They believed that the people in need could celebrate a new beginning and a reason to believe that the new year would bring blessings to them. This particular year was indeed special, since the family invited was bringing a very sad child to the party to try and cheer her through her difficult time. For at least two years, she would not talk, hardly ate, and cried most of each day. Because she had been in a terrible car accident, she lost her sisters and brothers, as well as both her legs. Her parents were desperate to save her, so they thought all of the animals would help her with her grief.

When the bright full sun of the day was starting to set, when all of the animals were cleaned and fed, when the house smelled of rich roast beef, buttered mashed potatoes, and pumpkin pie, the guests arrived. One by one, each of the animals greeted their ailing visitor. Pepper howled to the banjo, Sir Alex performed his happy dance, Sir Oliver grinned and strutted his show walk, Miss Tippi rolled over and danced on her hind legs, and Sir General rested his head in her lap. Nothing seemed to make a difference. She still cried and would not talk. The owners then wheeled her into the stable, where she saw Pokey hanging from his new branch, Ricky playing in his new maze, the kittens jumping on